the FAMOUSLY FUNNY PARROTT

the FAMOUSLY FUNNY PARROTT

FOUR TALES
from
THE BIRD
himself

Eric Daniel Weiner

Illustrated by Brian Biggs

DELACORTE PRESS

Text copyright © 2022 by Eric Daniel Weiner
Jacket art and interior illustrations copyright © 2022 by Brian Biggs

All rights reserved. Published in the United States by Delacorte Press, an imprint of Random House Children's Books, a division of Penguin Random House LLC, New York.

Delacorte Press is a registered trademark and the colophon is a trademark of Penguin Random House LLC.

Visit us on the Web! rhcbooks.com

Educators and librarians, for a variety of teaching tools, visit us at RHTeachersLibrarians.com

Library of Congress Cataloging-in-Publication Data is available upon request.
ISBN 978-0-593-37820-5 (hardcover)—
ISBN 978-0-593-37822-9 (ebook)

The text of this book is set in 11.75-point ITC Souvenir Std.

The illustrations were drawn with pencil on paper and digitally refined.
Interior design by THE COSMIC LION

Printed in the United States of America

10 9 8 7 6 5 4 3 2 1

First Edition

For Natalie,
for everything,
forever

Have I Got a Story for You!

(In Fact, I've Got Four of 'Em.)

the FAMOUSLY FUNNY PARROTT

the MYSTERY
of the
KNOCKING
DOOR

I don't know about you, but my favorite breakfast treat, by far, is the chocolate chip waffle.
I've had many sweet dreams about the chocolate
chip waffle. The dream is simple. There is a waffle
on a plate. I eat it.

Very early on Saturday, April tenth, of this year,
I was in the middle of one of these waffle dreams.
But just as I lifted fork to beak, I heard a terrible
knocking on my front door.

Knock-knock! Knock-knock-knock! Knock!

I tried to stay asleep, but I couldn't seem to fit all this knocking into my dream. A hammer kept smashing my breakfast plate to pieces.

I live in the Palm Court Arms in the cozy little town of Rubberwick, which is in the south of Vineland. Vineland is shaped rather like an iguana, is it not? We Rubberwickians like to say we live in the tip of the tail.

Now, take a close look at these pictures of my

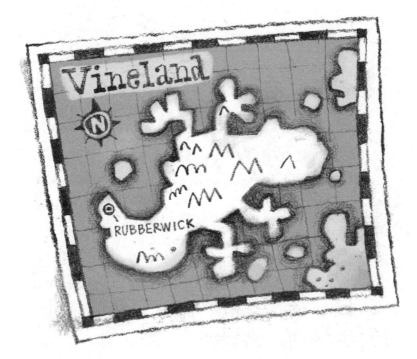

town. Do you *see* anything special happening in them? No, you don't! Because *nothing ever happens* in Rubberwick, which is just the way I like it. Nothing ever happens in the Palm Court Arms, either. It's a well-run, dignified building. In the mornings I can sleep as late as I like because it's blissfully quiet.

Not this morning.

Knock! Knock-knock! Knock-knock-knock!

I groaned. I stuck my head under four fluffy

pillows. I pressed the pillow pile down on my head with my wings. But I could still hear the person knocking.

"Who's there?" I called. But the only answer was another *KNOCK-KNOCK*.

"Knock-knock who?" I called.

Again, whoever was knocking answered by knocking some more.

I sat up with a sigh. "Peccary!" I called. I rang the big brass bell that I keep on the shelf beside my loft bed. "Peccary! Peccary!"

"Yes, sir?"

I was so startled I bonked my head on the rafters.

My butler has a terrible habit of appearing the instant I call him.

I peered down over the side of my bed. There stood Peccary, gazing up at me with his placid gray eyes. Ah, what a pleasingly furry face he has!

Thanks to the teensy bit of sunlight seeping through the windows, I could see that he had carefully combed the white whiskers under his chin. He was dressed, as always, in his wrinkle-free black suit. His black-and-white striped vest was buttoned tightly over his broad chest. His white silk handkerchief peeked out of his breast pocket. Stitched in green on the hankie was his monogram: *O.T.P.*

O.T.P. does not stand for *Oh, Tennis Partner.* It does not stand for *Omelet Tomato Pudding.* It stands for Oswald Theodore Peccary, the finest butler in the entire world.

"There seems to be someone at the front door, Peccary."

"Yes, sir."

Peccary clasped his hands behind his back, raised his long snout, and wiggled his round pink nose. Old O.T.P. seemed awfully awake and alert considering the hour, whatever that was.

"What time is it?" I said, rubbing my eyes.

Peccary consulted his pocket watch. "Six twenty-nine and thirty-seven seconds, sir."

"In the morning?"

"Indeed, sir."

"Who could be so rudely knocking at this hour? And more importantly, what the devil do they want?"

"I don't know."

"Well, have you checked?"

"Yes, sir. When the knocking began I immediately approached the door and said, 'Who's there?'"

"Sensible behavior, I must say."

"Thank you, sir. Since there was no response, I opened the door."

"Again, the most natural course of action."

"Yes, sir. But that is when I discovered that the answer to my question, 'Who's there?' was 'No one.'"

"I don't understand. Are you suggesting my front door is knocking all by itself?" I gave a wild laugh to show how silly a notion this was.

"Knock-knocking," said Peccary. "Quite so."

I clutched my cheeks with my wings. "Is it a ghost? Peccary, you know how terrified I am of ghosts. You're always assuring me there is no such thing."

"I continue to assure you," Peccary assured me.

"Well . . . how do we make the knocking stop?"

"I don't yet know."

A million butterflies fluttered in my quaking breast. Peccary? At a loss? What was the world coming to? And what was going to become of me? We Parrotts have always prided ourselves on our self-reliance. Personally, I pride myself on my reliance on Peccary.

"Well, Peccary, this is certainly unexpected."

"I'm terribly sorry for the disturbance, sir."

I rubbed my temples with my wing tips and whimpered. That rude *knock-knock*ing had not stopped. If anything, it had grown louder. It now sounded like this:

KNOCK KNOCK KNOCK

KNOCK

KNOCK KNOCK

"Well!" I said, with more bravado than I was feeling, "I'll just have to take care of this problem myself. You're a man of many skills, Peccary, but I guess even you can't solve everything. Here I come!"

I slid down the slide, which Peccary installed on

my loft bed after the seventeenth time I fell down the ladder.

As I slid, Peccary held out my fuzzy red slippers so that I'd slip right into them.

I am deeply fond of these fuzzy red slippers. I've had them for years. "Good morning, Snuggly. Good morning, Huggly," I said. Those are my pet names for left and right. I happily wiggled my eight toes inside them. "Sorry to wake you up so early, my pets. It seems we have a front-door crisis."

As I chatted with my slippers, Peccary helped

me with my white robe. He smoothed out the shoulders. They tend to bunch up over my wings.

My robe is monogrammed, just like Peccary's hankie, but my initials are stitched in purple, not green: *F.H.P.*

F.H.P. stands for me, Frederick Haven Parrott III, at your service.

And now, if you will follow me, as Peccary is doing, Snuggly, Huggly and I will shuffle along to my front door, and we will see to this *knock-knock*ing!

I padded down my purple-carpeted hallway, with Peccary following respectfully behind. I stopped short of entering the living room, however. Instead, I studied the old family portraits on the wall. You see, now that I was wide awake, the *knock-knock*ing sounded even more ominous than before. I shuddered. "Perhaps you had better go first, Peccary."

"Of course, sir."

"I'm only kidding, my good man," I said, sailing past him. "We Parrotts may not have filled the history books with acts of bravery. But certainly when the occasional front-door crisis arises we can, er, arise."

I stopped short again.

My living room is tastefully furnished in beiges and chestnuts and browns. On the left stands my wall-to-wall walnut bookcase. I am a devotee of great literature. The bookcase is stuffed from top

to bottom with my favorite comic books and joke books. In front of the bookcase is my comfy sofa, and in front of the sofa is my coffee table. On the right is the fireplace, next to which sits my easy chair and ottoman.

It's a lovely living room, and this morning all was just as it should be, except for my front door, which was knocking so hard it was rattling in its frame. Indeed, my front door was *knock-knock*ing so vigorously, the crystals of the chandelier in the marble foyer were *tinkle-tinkl*ing.

There are times in every parrot's life when he must face the music. In my case I had to face the knocking. I strode to the front door.

KNOCK-KNOCK!

"Who's there?" I demanded in a voice tinier than I intended.

KNOCK-KNOCK!

"Well, Peccary," I said, "I have figured out who is knocking. It's Mr. Knock-Knock. Isn't that right?" I said, turning to the door.

There was no answer except another dreadful *KNOCK!*

I grabbed the gold doorknob. I was about to fling open the door when I thought of a more cautious plan. I peeped through the peephole instead.

Instantly I was able to see that Peccary was right. There was no one there!

Bang! The door knocked so hard my head flew back like one of the toy robots in my Punch'em Kick'em Robot game.

I twisted my head back into position. "Well, you're right, Peccary, there's no one at the—"

I flung open the door as I cried, "Door!"

I looked left. I looked right. I even looked up and down.

No one there! I closed the door.

"This is quite the poser, Peccary." I leaned back against the door. I jumped off again before it could knock me for a loop.

"Ha-ha," I said, wagging my wing at the door. "Missed me that time!"

I bumped into the side table. On this table I keep a glass vase filled to the brim with bubble gum. I had to grab the vase to keep it from falling. I set it back down. No harm done.

"Yes," I continued, "this is truly a mystery. It's a mystery wrapped inside a conundrum, topped with a puzzle, and baked in an enigma."

"Indeed, sir."

"Now let's think, Peccary. Why would my front door begin to knock all of a sudden?"

Speaking of sudden, it suddenly hit me.

"I say, Peccary, isn't the doorknob of my front door . . . purple?"

Purple, as you may have guessed, is my favorite color. I'm purple-feathered with a patch of red on my neck like a napkin. All rather standard for a parrot. But I have three purple feathers on my head. I am very proud of these purple feathers. Everyone in my family has them. You might say it's the family crest. Right now my purple head feathers were fluttering nervously, but they were purple nonetheless, and at least when I had gone to bed, so was my doorknob.

"Come to think of it," I said, "was my front door always orange? A parrot may forget many things. Especially a parrot who ignored his butler's reminder that it was past his bedtime and stayed up late watching the National Tiddlywinks Tournament on TV. Rubberwick placed fourth, by the way."

"I am sorry to hear it, sir."

"Me too. But the point is, I'm sure that when I went to bed, my front door was Rainyforest Green."

"That part of the mystery is easily explained," said Peccary. He handed me a sheet of paper.

I'm a slow reader. I had to read the receipt several times. Once I absorbed it, though, the paper began to shake in my grip.

"Do you mean to tell me, Peccary, that while I was sleeping, you hired workmen to install a new front door?"

"Yes, sir."

RECEIPT

ONE DOOR
(installed by
Harold Sloth
& Sons)   1f

"Peccary, I've always counted on you to be levelheaded. Why on earth would you do such a thing?"

Peccary paused, as if considering how best to word his next statement. As it turned out, it was a shocker.

"You told me to do it, sir," said Peccary.

I don't know how long I stood in my front hall under the tinkling chandelier before I was able to respond.

"I told you to buy a new front door and have it installed while I was sleeping?!"

"Yes, sir," said Peccary, before I could exclaim, "Nonsense!"

"Why would I do that?"

"You said you were tired of the old front door. You thought it might be time for a bit of a refurbish. You said that if you had a new front door, who knows what you might open it to discover. You said a new front door would be the start of a grand adventure and a whole new lease on life."

"I said that?"

"You did indeed, sir."

"Was I awake at the time?"

"Yes, sir. But you might have been a bit under the influence of *The Constrictor Boys*."

Ah, *The Constrictor Boys*! The mere mention of *The Constrictor Boys* squeezed joy into my heart.

The Constrictor Boys, as I am sure I do not need to tell you, but which I will tell you anyway, is the wildly popular series of children's books by famed children's author Mabel Tapir. If you haven't read a *Constrictor Boys* book, put this book down and go remedy the situation at once.

Mabel Tapir's series is all about these two brave young boa constrictors, Jeff and Nick, and the mysteries they bravely solve. Brave brave brave are these brave boa brothers. In *The Great Front Doors,* the book I read most recently, or rather, the book Peccary most recently read to me, the boys were chasing after a greedy door manufacturer. It seems the bad door-maker had been selling overpriced front doors that fell to pieces the first time anyone knocked.

Peccary had finished reading the book to me last night. The stirring climax, which was stirring indeed, took place in a door factory. It was very hard for the Constrictor Boys to catch the bad guy. There were so many doors for him to hide behind. They caught him, though. The Constrictor Boys always get their man.

"That was quite the thrilling finale, Peccary."

"It was indeed, sir."

"You didn't happen to check out the next book in the series?"

"I am going to the library today."

"I can always count on you. But why did you listen to me when I told you to buy a new front door?" I whined.

"Because, sir, you said that if you didn't wake up this morning to find you had a new front door, then I should open the old front door and exit through it forever. Both from your life and your employ."

"I wasn't serious."

"You insisted that you were."

I blinked twice. *Blink-blink.* The mere thought of losing Peccary made my heart pound in rhythm with the knocking on the front door. It was as if someone were knocking both within and without.

"So when you fell asleep," continued my butler, "I phoned the nearest door store. I managed to reach them just before their own front doors closed. They said I was in luck. They said they had the most incredible front door on sale at a special low price. I should have been more suspicious. I'm dreadfully sorry, sir. All seemed fine while the workmen were here, installing the door. But as soon as they left, the door began to knock."

"Well, they'll just have to take it back."

RECEIPT

ONE DOOR
(installed by
Harold Sloth
& Sons)

1f

ABSOLUTELY
NO RETURNS

Peccary nodded at the receipt. At the bottom, stamped in large red letters, was the sentence *ABSOLUTELY NO RETURNS*.

I crumpled the receipt and threw it hard at the nearest wastebasket. A perfect shot, because Peccary went down the hall, fetched it, and dropped it right in.

"So what are we to do, Peccary?" I wailed. "Am I never to sleep again? Is my life ruined?"

I'm a firm believer that one should always stay calm in a crisis. I decided to make an exception. I began racing around the foyer shrieking.

I only stopped shrieking when confronted by an even greater horror. Peccary was gone.

He returned before I could shriek again. He was holding my toy tom-tom, which he had apparently fetched from my toy chest in the library.

"My tom-tom!" I cried, reaching for it happily. "Good thinking, Peccary. That little drum always calms me down."

"I will give it to you in a moment, sir," he said soothingly. "But I'd like to try something first, if I may."

"By all means."

He approached the quaking door and raised the drumstick. Lifting his snout and pursing his white lips, he looked off into the distance. He wrinkled that large flat nose of his several times. *Wrinkle-wrinkle.* And then at last he began to tom. He tom-tommed a series of short toms and long toms. Then he paused.

I paused, too. Not that I'd been doing anything. But I held my breath. Only then did I realize what else had paused. The orange door! It had ceased its knocking!

After a moment the door resumed knocking. But these weren't the loud, grim knocks that had shattered my dreams. These *knock-knock*s were softer.

"Ah," said Peccary. "Indeed." He tom-tommed some more. The door *knock-knock*ed its response. This went on for some time. It began to seem as if butler and front door were engaged in a rather unusual percussion duet.

"Peccary," I whispered. "What is going on?"

He smiled. "Good news, sir. Our mystery is solved."

"Tell me! Tell me!"

"I don't know why it didn't occur to me earlier. But it finally dawned on me that the door's knocking had a rather distinct rhythm. It was a sound that echoed down the chambers of memory. Finally I realized what it was: Morse code."

"Morse code! You know Morse code?"

"Yes, sir. It's from my navy days, don't you know."

"No, I don't know. You were in the navy?"

"I was engaged as the personal valet to Admiral Aardvark during the Great War of the Seashells. I was with him during the Battle of the Conch."

"Peccary, I'm not a scholar of naval history, but every schoolboy learns about the Battle of the Conch. It was won by Admiral Aardvark's brilliant tactical maneuvering. Something to do with raising and lowering the sails very rapidly, I believe."

"Exactly."

"You didn't, perchance, have something to do with that maneuver?"

"We do what we can, sir."

I felt a swell of pride. And this great man was my butler!

"A story for another time," I said, waving a wing. "Go on, dear Peccary. Tell me about the door."

"Yes, sir. I now know what the door has been trying to tell us."

"What?! What?!"

"Knock-knock jokes."

"Knock-knock jokes?"

"Indeed, sir. Apparently these are the door's favorite kind of jokes, since they involve someone knocking on a door."

"Well, that makes sense."

"Yes, sir. It claims to know a knock-knock joke for every name. Well, here. I bet the door would enjoy telling you a joke or two." He tapped on my tom-tom. "I'll translate; how does that sound?"

"It sounds marvelous."

KNOCK-KNOCK went the door.

"Knock-knock," said Peccary.

"I don't think you need to translate that part," I pointed out.

"Quite so."

Peccary drummed and said, "Who's there?"

"Orange" was the door's response.

"Orange who?" asked Peccary.

"Orange you glad I'm orange?" knocked the door.

To be totally honest, I wasn't sure how glad

I was. A joke-telling front door might take some getting used to.

Meanwhile, the door began knocking out joke after joke. He even told one with my first name!

Knock-knock.

Who's there?

Freddie.

Freddie who?

Freddie or not, here I come!

"Freddie or not, here I come!" I repeated, slapping my side. "I like that. Ooh, ooh, does the door know one for my middle name?"

Peccary tapped out the request and the door responded at once.

Knock-knock.

Who's there?

Haven.

Haven who?

Haven you heard me knocking?

I was getting quite giggly. "Your name, Peccary, your name!"

Knock-knock.

Who's there?

Oswald.

Oswald who?

Oswald a fly!

"I don't get it," I said.

"Try saying it out loud, sir," suggested Peccary, "and say it slowly."

"Oswallld a flyyyy. . . . I swallowed a fly! I get it now, and now that I get it, I find it highly amusing. Your middle name!" I cried, clapping.

Knock-knock.

Who's there?

Theodore.

Theodore who?

Theodore is stuck! Open up!

And so it went, one nutty knock-knock joke after another. You know how it is with jokes, especially silly ones: the more you tell 'em, the funnier they get. Peccary is not a big laugher, historically. But even he began to chuckle.

We must have made a rather silly sight, me and my butler, dancing around the foyer, Peccary drumming and both of us shouting out jokes. At last, all this fun and laughter began to tire me out. Sweet sleepiness poured over me like syrup over a chocolate-chip waffle.

I yawned and said, "Peccccccary, now that we—er, you—have solved the knock-knock mystery"—I yawned again—"excuuuuuuse me! I think I shall toddle off back to bed."

"A fine plan, sir."

"Just one question. How did my front door manage to learn Morse code? I'm shocked enough that you knew it."

"Well, sir, it's rather a sad story."

"Oh?"

"It seems our young door loves knock-knock jokes so much, it keeps knocking wherever it goes. Most people don't like a knocking door, sir. Even though the store refuses to give people their money back, customers return the door immediately. As a result, this young door has already had many owners. It once lived at a telegraph office, which is where it picked up Morse code. But even in the telegraph office, no one understood what all its knocking was about."

"But you figured it out, my brilliant butler. Well played, my little tom-tom."

"Thank you, sir."

I stretched my wings and yawned more deeply.

"But why was the door *knock-knock*ing all morning? There's a time and a place for everything. I myself enjoy knock-knock jokes much more when I'm awake."

"The door says it's very sorry. It was just excited to meet us. It promises it won't happen again. It begs you not to return it to the store like all the previous owners have done."

This pulled on the old heartstrings, I must say. I went up to the door. I cleared my throat. I felt a little foolish, addressing my own front door. I glanced back at my butler. "Translate for me, will you, Peccary?"

"Of course." Peccary raised his drumstick.

"Knock-Knock Door," I said, "you old knockety-knock, you. Your troubles are over. I wouldn't dream of returning you, not for all the cocoa on the island of Canoe. And apparently Canoe has a lot of cocoa. I mean to say, how many other people can boast of having a funny front door? Nobody."

I waited while Peccary tom-tommed.

After a brief silence, the door knocked back. I looked to Peccary.

"It thanks you, sir, from the bottom of its door-y heart."

"Aww!" I signaled for Peccary to drum. "Knock-knock!" I said.

"Who's there?" knocked my door.

"Isadora."

"Isadora who?"

"Is—adora my new door's new name? Yes it is, you adorable door."

It took Peccary a while to drum all that.

Adora knocked back softly.

"Knock-knock," Peccary translated.

"Who's there?" cried I.

"Boo."

"Boo who?"

"Boo-hoo-hoo-hoo."

"Oh my," said Peccary. "You've moved the door to tears."

I like to put on a stern front, stiff upper beak, don't you know. But inside my parrot body lurks a heart of mush. What I did next, I tell you without the least bit of shame. I kissed my own front door.

"Adora, you are my front door forevermore," I whispered, and Peccary gently drummed my sentiment.

the CASE
of the
MISSING
WAFFLE
BATTER

It was morning. Well, it was one in the afternoon, but I had just woken up, so I call that morning, and morning calls for breakfast, and breakfast calls for waffles. I was sitting in the dining room in my bathrobe and slippers. You know the ones. Good old Snuggly and Huggly. My purple napkin was tied around my neck, my knife and fork were in hand, but my plate was still empty.

"I want a waffle! I want a waffle!" I chanted,
banging on the table with my knife and fork.

"I'm so sorry for the delay, sir," said Peccary.

Yikes! My excellent butler had popped out of
the kitchen like a jack-in-the-box. I was so startled
I threw my silverware in the air.

Knife and fork clattered to the floor. The knife spun in noisy circles like a top.

"I wish you wouldn't sneak up on me like that, Peccary."

"Sorry, sir." Peccary was wearing his frilly omelet-colored apron. This apron always adds a nice breakfast-y air to his formal black suit. But his expression this morning wasn't breakfast-y at all.

I peered at him closely. "Why the gloomy face, my good man? Surely a little dropped cutlery isn't the end of the world?"

Peccary bent down and picked up the knife and fork. He dropped them into the front pocket of his apron. "That isn't why I'm frowning, sir."

Still frowning, he floated over to the sideboard and selected a new knife and fork.

"Well, why are you frowning, then?"

He studied the fork, polished it a bit with the corner of his apron, then set it down in perfect parallel to my plate. "I'm afraid it's your morning waffles, sir."

My three purple head feathers stood up straight.

"My morning waffles? What about my morning waffles?"

"It seems there's no batter, sir."

"No batter? But that's impossible. You prepared the batter last night. You told me so at bedtime. I couldn't sleep till you had double- and triple-checked."

"And so I did, sir."

"So?"

"It is now gone, sir."

"Gone?!"

"Indeed, sir. The bowl is licked clean."

"Oh, my! Do you mean to say it's been—stolen?"

"That wouldn't be my first conclusion, sir. I believe someone has eaten it."

"The plot thickens," I said. "Whom do you suspect?"

"You, sir."

"*Me?!*"

"Yes, sir."

"Peccary, I can't say I like the way your suspicions always seem to land on me. Why, I recall a time when you accused me of making you buy a new door in the middle of the night."

"But that was what you had done, sir."

"Yes, I know, but that isn't the point I'm trying to make."

"What point are you trying to make?"

"I don't remember but I'll make a different one, how's that?" I crossed my wings firmly over my chest. I forgot I had picked up the fork. "Ow!"

I tossed the fork back onto the table. "I can assure you with one hundred percent confidence that I did not eat the waffle batter."

Peccary looked unconvinced.

"I give you my word as a gentleman," I added.

Still the man looked dubious.

To make my point more emphatically, I stood from my chair and raised a wing in the air. "I, Frederick Haven Parrott the Third, did not eat the waffle batter. I would swear to it in a court of law."

"I believe you are telling the truth, sir."

"Thank you." I sat back down.

"As far as you know it."

"Peccary, you sphinx! What do you mean by that remark?"

"I believe you ate the batter while you were asleep, sir."

"While I was *asleep!*"

"Yes, sir. You sometimes sleepwalk, as you know."

This was true. Before Peccary began triple-locking our front door at night, he once found me in the garden behind our building, gazing up at the moon.

"All right, so I sleepwalk. What of it?"

"Sometimes you also sleep eat."

"Sleep *eat*?"

"Yes, sir. It's a rare phenomenon but not un-heard of. Since I'm aware of this danger, I usually padlock the fridge before retiring. Last night I forgot. I'm very sorry, sir."

"Interesting theory, Peccary, but have you any proof?"

"No, sir. But I feel quite confident of my conclusion. Our front door reports that it remained locked all night. Nobody knocked except itself. You and I are the only residents of apartment three K. I didn't eat the batter. I'm afraid this leaves us with only one suspect."

"Well, you're wrong. We've been robbed, Peccary. Robbed! The thing to do is call the police."

"The police, sir?"

"Exactly."

"I'm not sure that would be advisable, sir."

"Why not?"

"The police are usually rather busy."

"With what, Peccary? With solving crimes and

44

catching criminals, is that not so? Of course it is.
And if stealing waffle batter doesn't count as a
crime I don't know what does."

"May I remind you, sir, that the last time we
called the police it was because you couldn't find
your purple sippy straw. The straw turned out to
be stuck in your top feathers. You and the police

quarreled. I believe it was those two local officers who ride around on large black horses—Officer Scott Piranha and Officer Gladys Otter. They ended up giving you a rather stiff fine. Then there was the time—"

"Yes, yes. Spare me the history lesson, Peccary, if you don't mind."

Sometimes one has to take a firm tone with Peccary. I don't mind being chummy with my butler, but there comes a time when one must draw a line in the sandbox, as they say. The time, I believed, was now.

"Peccary, call the police this second. End of discussion."

"Very good, sir."

After he phoned the police, Peccary went about his duties. First he prepared my consolation-prize breakfast: fresh-squeezed orange juice, big buttered muffins with lots of strawberry jam, creamy scrambled eggs and bacon, crunchy hash browns and a lollipop.

Each delicious bite or lick was a fresh slap in the face, for it reminded me of what it was not: a

chocolate chip waffle. When my heart is set, no substitutes will do. I'm sure you feel the same.

After breakfast, I wandered around my apartment, playing with my sparkly blue yo-yo. The yo-yo went up and down but my mood remained down. I was still smarting from Peccary's accusation of waffle thievery.

I hate being accused. Being accused of something I might have done is even worse.

As I yo-yoed, I tried to think of something I could accuse Peccary of having done. That's the problem with Peccary: he never gives me anything to be angry about. It makes me furious.

It's not easy to yo-yo while you walk. At least,

it's not easy for some. Sorry to boast, but I'm a yo-yo pro. Why, I can even skip and yo-yo at the same time. I did so now. Upping the difficulty factor a notch further, I put my yo-yo to sleep.

You know the sleeper trick. You let the yo-yo rest at the end of its string before pulling it back up. When I entered the living room, the yo-yo had been sleeping for what seemed to be a record amount of time. I tripped slightly. The yo-yo woke with a vengeance, shot up and bashed me on the chin.

We Parrotts are tough birds. My yo-yo wasn't going to knock me down for the count. On the count of nineteen I was standing once more.

Peccary was sweeping up something at my feet. "What are you up to now, then?" I said.

"These brown bits flew off your chin when you received the blow from the yo-yo, sir."

"Brown bits? They're not part of my chin, are they?" Gingerly I felt my bottom beak.

"No, sir, it's—"

"Well, never mind," I interrupted.

For quite a while now, I'd been hearing strange *clippity-cloppy* sounds. I massaged my temples.

"Is there something wrong, sir?"

"I'm beginning to think I might have done some damage to my hearing when I yo-yoed myself in the face."

"Shall I get you some ice, sir?"

"Perhaps. But didn't you say something fell off my chin when the yo-yo struck?"

He held up the dustbin. "I have examined the detritus, sir. It's bits of dried waffle."

"Dried waffle? How would bits of dried waffle get on my chin while I was sleeping?!"

"Excuse me," said Peccary, "if I may—"

"Of course."

He gave the red feathers on my neck a quick *whisk-whisk*.

"After all," I said, "I haven't eaten any waffles this morning and—"

Peccary was still holding the dustbin. I was looking at the dried brown bits of waffle that had come from my chin, along with the dried brown bits of waffle he had just whisked from my feathers. That's when it hit me with the force of a speeding yo-yo. There was only one way those dried bits of waffle could have gotten onto my chin during the night.

"Well, Peccary," I said. "I guess it's time to forgive you for accusing me of committing waffle thievery while asleep."

"I'm grateful to hear it, sir."

"Also it might be time to phone the police and suggest they need not come, after all. You can tell them that since they have been so slow in arriving, we've been forced to solve the crime ourselves."

"Hmm. I'm afraid it may be a little late for—"

My darling front door, Adora, interrupted Peccary with a loud *knock-knock*.

"Who's there?" I called out.

"Police!"

"Police who?"

"Police open the door!"

"Ha," I said. "That's a funny one! I've heard many knock-knocks in my time but I don't think I've heard that one before. *Police* open the door. Priceless!"

Knock-knock!

Adora knocked quite a bit louder this time. Apparently, the door had a second joke that it was even more excited to tell me.

"Who's there?" I cried as I danced around the living room.

"Police!"

"Police who?"

"Police stop telling stupid knock-knock jokes and open the door!"

51

This gave me pause. It wasn't Adora's style of humor.

Before I had time to puzzle over Adora's second joke, however, the door fired off a third.

KNOCK-KNOCK!

In retrospect, I can see that it was my dancing about the room that distracted me. I wasn't paying enough attention to what Peccary was doing, which was opening the door.

"Who's there?" I cried. "Scott," I answered myself. "Scott who? Scott's nothing to do with me, but that Officer Scott Piranha is one of the most simpleminded officers I've ever met!"

"Uh, sir?"

"Knock-knock!" I cried. "Who's there? Gladys. Gladys not the police because the police are a bunch of dunces, especially that Officer Gladys Otter!"

"Sir!"

"Yes, Peccary?"

"There are some people here to see you, sir."

"Oh?" I had my back turned. I was afraid to look. "Who's there?" I inquired meekly.

"It's the police."

"Police who?" I said, with one last stab at humor. Slowly I turned. Holding a wing to my eye, I peeked through my feathers.

What I saw first were two pairs of dark leather riding boots. I lowered my wing and thus got a more complete picture. In the doorway stood two uniformed officers, Officer Scott Piranha and Officer Gladys Otter.

I keep a vase filled with bubble gum on the table next to Adora. It's my way of welcoming guests. "Care for some bumble gum?" I asked as I held up the vase. "I mean, er, bubble gum?"

When the officers didn't answer, I added, "It's Dr. Toucan Triple Bubble, with a little cartoon inside each one." I raised the vase again.

Officer Piranha waved me away with an orange fin. "Your butler said you wanted to see us?"

"Yes," I said. "But before we get to that, I think *I* will indulge in a piece of gum, if you don't mind." I took one, then two, then three pieces of bubble gum, unwrapped them, slipped the little comic inserts into my robe pocket so that I could peruse them later, shoved all the gum into my mouth and started chewing hard.

"So? What's the problem?" demanded Officer Otter.

"Well, you see, Officers—sorry, hard to talk with all this gum in my mouth." I popped in a fourth piece. I added a fifth and a sixth. Then I turned to Peccary for support.

The man had vanished.

What was the matter with Peccary this morning? First it was accuse, accuse. Now he was acting as if, having opened the door, he had completed his duties. I'd have to speak to him about that. But first, I popped in bubble gum pieces seven and eight.

"I'll tell you what happened . . ." I began chewing piece of gum number nine. I placed the vase back on the table. "That's enough out of you!" I said, taking just one last piece. I turned back to face the coppers with a big sunny smile. Well, not so sunny. It was hard to open my beak with all that gum in it. I stepped out into the hall so I could speak to the police more quietly, which at the moment was the only way I could speak to them.

"It's really"—*chew-chew*—"quite an amusing story," I mumbled, "if you look at it from the right angle."

Officer Piranha removed his police helmet and scratched his head. "Look, mate, I like funny stories as much as the next fellow. But is it on the short side? We're rather busy."

"Oh, it's very short. Now, let's see. What shall I call my very amusing and very short story? I think I'll call it—"

Before I could think of a title, the door to the

apartment next to mine cracked open. Two long hairy snouts stuck out.

3L is home to my nosy neighbors, Alfred and Anita Anteater. I'm used to these two old busy-bodies sticking their long snouts out their door and into my business. But these two snouts were coming from lower down. It was the Anteaters' five-year-old twin grandchildren, Aaron and Allison.

Whenever they visit, Aaron and Allison amuse themselves by making my life miserable. Pushing all the buttons when I get on the elevator, gluing the morning paper to the welcome mat, sneaking up behind me and shouting "Boo!" so that I leap about and call for my mama—these were just a few of their favorite pastimes. Today they employed a more painful trick.

Please do not try this at home unless you're an anteater. Apparently, Aaron and Allison had stuck lots of uncooked peas up their noses. Now they fired away. *Pfft! Pfft! Pfft!*

After they shot me, they quickly and quietly closed the door.

I jumped and growled, "Stop it, you brats!"

Officers P&O exchanged glances.

"That's the title of the story?" asked Officer Otter, her eyes narrowing.

"What? Oh, ha-ha, no. It's these two little neighbors of mine. Look!" But of course when they looked, the door to 3L was closed, and my young neighbors were nowhere to be seen. "Those pesky preschoolers. I can never seem to catch them in the act."

"Look, Parrott," said Officer Otter. "Like Officer Piranha said, we're very busy."

"Yeah," agreed Officer P. "So if you have a funny story, let's have it."

I got it, all right. The door to 3L opened and I received another fusillade of peas.

I'm not proud of the next words that came out of my mouth. I was under great stress, however. Despite all the gum clogging up my beak, I managed to shriek, "Leave me alone, you filthy idiots!"

"Ah, geez," said Officer Piranha. He reached into his right pants pocket and withdrew a black-bound notebook. "I'm sorry, Parrott. But that's going a bit far."

Uh-oh.

I knew this notebook. The last time it came out of Officer Piranha's pocket, it cost me fifty furthings.

"Parrott, you leave me no choice," said Officer Piranha. He began filling out the form with a stubby red pencil. With my super parrot vision, I focused in on the letters on the side of the pencil. Police pencils usually say *R.P.D.*, as in, Rubberwick Police Department. On this little pencil, only the *P.D.* remained.

I knew what that spelled. Parrot Doom.

"Calling officers names. One hundred furthings."

"*What?!*"

"Sticks and stones will break my bones," chimed in Officer Otter. "You call us names and you'll get fined."

"No. Please. This is a simple misunderstanding. I would never call you names. I mean, I know I called you some recently, but I thought the door was closed. Anyway, I was speaking to my neighbors. They're just little children, you see. Here, I'll show you!"

I was going to open the door to 3L and catch the little varmints red-handed. They opened the

60

door for me. *Pfft! Pfft! Pfft! Pfft! Pfft! Pfft! Pfft! Pfft! Pfft! Pfft!*

They had really stuffed their noses this time. As they *pfft*ed, I danced. "Stop it! Stop it! Stop it at once! You're a couple of little barbarians, you know that?"

I yelled all this at 3L, but that didn't seem to keep the police from taking it personally.

"That'll be two hundred furthings," said Officer Piranha, crossing out the original number.

"What? No no no!" I cried, stomping up and down.

Unfortunately, thanks to all this stomping, my robe untied itself.

Under the robe I was wearing a pair of blazingly bright blue bloomers. This particular pair was decorated with red tomatoes that dance around with top hats and canes. I'm actually quite fond of this pair of underwear, but it's not meant for police consumption.

"Showing off your underpants, eh?" said Officer Piranha.

"Mighty fine bloomers," agreed Officer Otter. "But there's a law against strutting around in public in your underpants. Add one hundred furthings to his fine, Officer P."

"What? No! No! You mustn't add any more to that fine. You mustn't!"

As I pleaded my case, I tried to retie my robe. Usually I can tie my robe and chew gum at the same time. Not this time.

After all, I had really stuffed quite a bit of gum into the old beak. Without even realizing what I was doing, I began to blow a bubble.

I'm even better at bubble-blowing than I am at yo-yoing. In fact, I'd go so far as to say I'm a bubble-blowing expert. I once came in eighth in Rubberwick's annual bubble-blowing contest. I have a trophy on my mantel to prove it. *Eighth Place out of Eight.* It says it right on the base.

Anyway, this morning's bubble would have won me first prize. I could see the police officers' eyes widening as the bubble got larger and larger. Soon I could only see the bubble. That's how large it had become.

We shall never know what record-breaking size that bubble might have reached. Because just then—

Pfft! Pfft! Pfft! Pfft! Pfft! Pfft! Pfft! Pfft! Pfft! Pfft! Pfft! Pfft! Pfft! Pfft! Pfft! Pfft! Pfft!

From behind me came round number four from the pea-shooters. The twins nailed me right in the bum with seventeen peas. This caused me to jump. And when I landed . . .

POPPPPPPPPPPPPPPPPPPP!!!!!!!!!!!!!!!!!!!!!

Slowly and quietly, I closed and locked Adora. Peccary stood by the fireplace, dusting that bubble-blowing trophy of mine. That trophy was the last thing I wanted to see. Peccary, on the other hand, is the first thing I want to see whenever trouble hits.

"Peccary," I moaned. I handed him the fine.

"Oh, dear," he said. "Oh dear dear dear."

"It's such a big fine," I said tearfully.

"It is on the large side, sir," agreed Peccary.

"Five hundred furthings, for popping my gum all over the police officers' faces."

I looked at Peccary, those calm gray eyes. "Peccary," I said, sniffling. "You were right. We never should have called the police."

"Now, now. What's done is done."

My butler handed me his hankie and I blew my

nares, as we parrots say. Nares are the little holes on the sides of our beaks. Peccary has a funny word for his nares. He calls the holes in his big pink nose *nostrils.*

I leaned against him for support. He patted my back. "There, there."

I peered up at him.

"Peccary?"

"Sir?"

"Do you know what would cheer me up at this moment?"

"What is that, sir?"

"A chocolate chip waffle. With whipped cream on top and maple syrup flowing all over it and . . ."

"Um . . ."

"Make me a waffle, Peccary! Make me a waffle right now!"

The look on his face showed me there was a problem. An instant later I remembered what it was.

"Oh no!" I sobbed. "Our waffle batter has been stolen! By me!" I buried my face in my wings.

When I looked up, there was a twinkle in Peccary's eye. The man was trying not to laugh, I could tell. He didn't succeed. Peccary began to guffaw.

I was shocked. I was outraged. But I was also amused. Peccary has a very contagious laugh, on those rare occasions when he uses it. Soon I too was howling with laughter.

"*Snort! Snort!*" went Peccary.

That happens to the man sometimes. He laughs so hard he snorts.

"*Snort! Snort!*"

There, you see, he did it again. This made us both laugh even harder.

"They did look pretty funny with gum all over their faces." I giggled.

"I'm sure they did, sir," said Peccary, in between snorts and guffaws.

"Perhaps it was even worth the fine," I mused, when we had both calmed down at last.

"Perhaps it was indeed, sir," agreed Peccary, smiling at me. Then he gave another snort and we laughed anew.

Ah, Peccary. He had done it again. No matter how much trouble I get into, he always makes everything all right in the end.

a VERY WINDY WEDNESDAY

This past Wednesday, September seventeenth, was a very windy Wednesday indeed. Gusts of cold wind rattled the windows of my apartment like castanets. It was, I thought, the perfect day for a drive.

You see, when I'm not staying home all day, as I usually do, when I'm not sleeping very late or going to bed very early, when I'm not in my easy chair in my jammies giggling over a comic book, I can be quite the adventurer.

Yes, I thought. *Time to take my roadster for a spin.* I made it as far as the front door.

"Just one moment, sir," called my butler, Peccary.

As always, he was dressed just so in his wrinkle-free black suit and black-and-white-striped vest. For some reason he was carrying an extra pair of shoes.

I recognized these shoes. They were my milk-chocolate-brown dress shoes. I had already put on

the tasteful three-piece brown suit he had selected for my outing. My rainbow-colored spangly outfit with the horn-shaped buttons that actually honk, that was my first choice. Peccary insisted that suit was a bit loud.

"Well, what is it now, Peccary?"

"I just thought you might want to change out of your slippers, sir."

I looked down. "Ah, yes."

"Don't worry," I told my fuzzy red slippers as Peccary removed first left (Snuggly) then right (Huggly). "I will be home again soon, my pets. I just want to tootle around Rubberwick a bit. See the pretty leaves as they change colors. Enjoy the crisp fall air."

Peccary flipped the tail of his black suit jacket out of his way as he knelt. He began tying my shoelaces in double knots. "Have you got your driver's license, sir?" he asked with his head down.

"No, I do not," I answered factually.

Peccary returned in a flash with the license in hand.

I could tell he had something more to say. "Well?" I said. "Out with it, my good man."

Peccary tapped his paws together lightly. "I was just thinking, sir, it is a very windy Wednesday."

"A weather report, eh?"

"Yes, sir. On very windy days such as these, I think it advisable to drive your convertible with its top closed."

"Oh, pshaw," I said. "Do you see what is on my head?"

"You are wearing your driving cap, sir."

"Correct. I love this driving cap, Peccary. The orange and white checks remind me of carrot cake with cream cheese icing. This cap keeps my head warm even with the top of my car— Er . . . what is wrong with Adora?"

My front door, Adora, had begun knocking with great excitement.

"Your front door wants to tell you a knock-knock joke, sir," explained Peccary.

Peccary always keeps my toy tom-tom handy so he can communicate with Adora in Morse code. Peccary drummed and translated as my front door knock-knocked.

Knock-knock.

Who's there?

Augusta.

Augusta who?

Augusta wind could blow your driving cap right out of the car.

"Not a bad joke," I said. "I must remember to tell it to my Great Aunt Augusta. Well now, Peccary, you and the door have made your point. Top closed. Got it. And now—"

I put my hand on my front door's golden doorknob, but Peccary's expression gave me pause.

"Did you have yet another caution?" I asked, rather testily.

"Yes, sir."

"Well, caution away, Peccary. While we stand here gabbing, the whole pretty fall day is flying by, and I have yet to enjoy a leaf of it."

"I wanted to remind you about that sharp turn off Rubberwick Avenue onto Duck Pond Lane, sir."

"Oh, that *is* a nasty turn," I agreed with a chuckle. "It's right by the mansion of that awful friend of mine, Lord Norton Bush Dog. Do you know, Peccary, I sometimes imagine Norton spends the day gazing out the windows of his mansion like a spider in his web, hoping to see an accident."

I leaned casually against the wall. It seems I was a bit farther from the wall than I thought. I fell over with a crash.

"I am not overly fond of that particular chum of yours," said Peccary, helping me back to my feet. "But my point remains: use caution on that turn."

"Right-o," I said. "Top closed and snail speed on the turn! Please drum my goodbye to Adora for me."

And with that I sailed out the door and down the hallway. As I sailed, I could hear Peccary drumming my message to Adora, and Adora knocking back. Soon I was on the elevator, hurtling upward on my new adventure. Did I say upward? Oh dear, I pressed the wrong button. Well, no harm done.

Outside the Palm Court Arms is a large portico. The portico is held up by green pillars that are shaped like palm trees. In his green uniform and top hat, our doorman looks like a pillar of a palm tree himself. As you can see, Justin Caiman is a scaly old green alligator. He seems to have forgotten how to smile.

"Good morning, Justin," I said.

"Good morning, sir. Though more of an after-noon, I'd say. It is after three."

"Good point, Justin. Now, if you would ask Abbot to bring round my—"

Wheels crunched on gravel.

The valet at the Palm Court is a pale green toad by the name of Abbot Suriname. Here he came now, driving up in my Red Arrow.

"Well, that was quick," I said.

"Your butler phoned down and instructed us to bring your car round from the garage, sir."

The man thinks of everything.

Ah, the Red Arrow. Feast your eyes on this shiny red beast. I got behind the wheel. I turned

the key. *VROOM-VROOM* went the Red Arrow's powerful V-29 double-banger engine. I honked the little horn. *Beep! Beep!* Then I honked the big one.

AHOOOGAAAAAA!

AHOOOGAAAAAA!

AHOOOGAAAAAA!

AHOOOGAAAAAA!

AHOOOGAAAAAA!

By my fifth *ahoogaa* I noticed that Justin and Abbot had their fingers in their ears. Well, time to be off.

"Ta-ta!" I called.

There is a button on the dash of my convertible that closes its top with a *zoop*. I zooped it. I didn't like being closed in, however. *Zoop!* I opened the top again.

Peccary had told me to close it, and Adora agreed with him. *Zoop!* I closed the top.

But Peccary wasn't *always* right. And what did my front door know about driving? *Zoop!* I opened the top again. This time I left it open.

I drove round the semicircular driveway, looked both ways, then pulled out onto Rubberwick Avenue.

My, the wind was strong! It was so gusty that

leaves were flying everywhere, off on little adventures of their own, I suppose.

Rubberwick Avenue is a wide and stately street, dotted on either side by the occasional mansion. Suddenly the whole right side of the street vanished completely. Then the left side disappeared as well!

I realized what the problem was. Two large leaves had plastered themselves onto my face. It was as if I had donned a sleep mask and gone nighty-night.

AHHHHHHHHHHHHH!!!!!!

The car swerved from side to side as I struggled to peel off the leaves. Thinking quickly, I lifted my foot and stomped on the brake. Since I couldn't see a thing, was it my fault that I stomped on the gas?

The car shot forward.

I peeled the leaves from my eyes and grabbed the wheel. I stopped the car from swerving. But now I found myself zooming into that sharp turn that Peccary had been so fussy about, the turn off Rubberwick Avenue onto Duck Pond Lane.

I made the turn expertly, considering the high speed at which I was hurtling. How could I have prepared for what happened next?

It was as if the universe itself was telling knock-knock jokes.

Just as I rounded the bend, *Augusta* wind caught my driving cap. The powerful wind lifted my cap right off my head. I grabbed for my cap. But the cap kept darting out of my reach. At last the cap landed—right on my face.

Ahhhhhhhhhhhhhhhhhhhhhhhhhhhhhhhhhhhhh-hhhhhhhhhhhhhh!!!

Have you ever driven with your hat over your

face? I don't recommend it. It gives you a warm fuzzy feeling but you can't see a thing.

I whipped off the cap.

I had been blinded only for a split second. But during that split second I had driven right up close to another car!

It was an expensive car, the most expensive kind of car there is: a big black-and-silver Rolly Royce. The Royce was parked well out into the roadway. The driver's-side door was hanging open. White smoke puffed out the tailpipe. The license plate? *LORD BUSH DOG RULES!*

In that same split second I saw that the road was clear, no oncoming traffic. Instantly I knew what I had to do. I had to swerve dramatically left, then right.

I swerved left. I swerved right.

I zigzagged perfectly, I must say.

Well, if we're going to get all nitpicky about my zigzagging, I zagged a bit too far. I was now driving at an odd angle along the banks of the pond, right down by the water's edge.

Up ahead I saw something that silly Rolly had previously blocked from view. Two police officers

were sitting on two big black horses. The officers were letting their horses take a drink from the pond.

I recognized these two police officers. It was Officer Scott Piranha and Officer Gladys Otter. I have run into these two officers more often than I would like. This time I was about to run into them with my car.

Both officers turned. Their faces took on sort of horrified expressions.

I jammed down on the brakes. I blasted the horn.

AHOOOOOOOOOOOOOOOOOOOOOOOOOO OOOOOOOOOOOOGAAAAAAAAAAAAAAAA AAAAAAAA!!!!

I screeched to a halt right behind the horses. Well done, Freddie!

Unfortunately, the startled horses bucked with all their might.

Up, up flew the officers. And as so often happens with up, up, this was quickly followed by down, down.

SPLOOSH!

SPLOOSH!

I have a bad habit of not leaping into action in an emergency. Sometimes, like now, I simply stare at the scene with an open beak.

My beak was still in the wide-open position as Officers P and O climbed out of the pond. It's a good thing I don't believe in sea monsters, or I might not have recognized them. They were covered with green plants and dark oozy mud.

Officer Piranha emptied out his helmet. A little yellow fish dove back into the pond. Officer Otter twisted her right pants leg. Water gushed out. And I started——

Laughing?

That's not like me. I would never laugh at another's misfortune. At least, not right in front of them.

After all, people don't like being laughed at. Police officers who have just been catapulted into duck ponds are especially touchy.

"You think this is funny, Parrott?" said Officer Piranha. "Fine! As in—!"

He whipped out a black notebook. It was covered with seaweed, but I recognized this object all too well. It was his book of fines!

"No, no, no," I said. "I wasn't laughing. I promise you."

But then I laughed even harder—and louder! I went cross-eyed. Had my beak developed a new trick of laughing all by itself?

Then I saw where the laughter was coming from. Do you remember that the duck pond is right near the mansion of my "friend" Lord Norton Bush Dog? And do you also remember that when I did my zigzag maneuver I went round my filthy rich chum's Rolly Royce?

Well, I can put two and two together as well as the next fellow. Two plus two equals Norton. Sure enough, he now climbed out of his car, laughing. He was doubled over, he was laughing so hard.

Allow me to introduce you. Lord Bush Dog.

Still laughing, he whipped his red silk handkerchief from the breast pocket of his blue blazer. He blew on the lenses of his glasses, then carefully wiped them. They went *squeak squeak*. At least, I assume they went *squeak squeak*. Mostly I heard Norton howling.

"You see?" I told the police. "I wasn't the one who was laughing. I'm so, so sorry, by the way. Thank goodness you are both okay!"

"Yes, officers, sorry for laughing," said Norton. "But it's not every day you get to see police officers go flying into the duck pond. Ha-ha-ha!"

Both officers crossed their arms.

"But," Norton went on, giggling in a high pitch, "that wasn't the funniest thing. Freddie here was driving with a hat over his face. Ha-ha-ha! That's why he knocked you into the pond."

"Is that true, Parrott?" demanded Officer Otter.

"Well, yes, but it was only for a second. You see—"

"Driving with hat over face," said Officer Piranha as he wrote out my fine.

I sighed. "Well, I suppose I deserve a, er, tiny fine?"

"You deserve a bigger fine than that," said Norton. "Sorry to tell you this, officers, but he was speeding."

"Speeding on a dangerous turn," said Officer Piranha, "with hat over face."

"Oh, dear! It was so funny," giggled Norton. "He was waving his wings and doing the Hokey Pokey. Like this!" Norton waved his arms and staggered around the banks of the pond.

"Doing Hokey Pokey," said Officer Piranha, scribbling.

"I was not doing the Hokey Pokey!" I said. I searched for a clever response. "What a jokey!"

"Jokey Hokey Pokey," said Officer Piranha, still writing.

"Sorry, Freddie," said Norton, coming round to my side of the car. "I hope I haven't gotten you

into any trouble. Oh, look, you have a spot of waffle on your feathers."

I looked down. Norton zipped his finger up my
chest and tweaked my beak. "Gotcha!" he said.
More high-pitched giggling.

Just then, something in the rearview mirror
caught my eye.

It was such a welcome sight, I had to turn my
head to make sure it was true.

It was true.

The Rolly Royce had begun to roll. It was rolling slowly down the bank toward the pond.

"I say, Norton, I hate to spoil your fun. But you might want to do something about your car."

"My car? Why?"

He looked where I was looking. "No, no, no! Stop, Rolly! Stop!" he cried, waving his arms. He raced after the rolling car.

Now who's doing the Hokey Pokey? I thought.

The Rolly Royce picked up speed. It bumped up and down over the grassy slope. Then the car hit a really big bump.

The big fancy car lifted high into the air. It was almost as if all its life the Rolly Royce had wanted to swim with the ducks.

SPLOOOOOOOOOOOOOOOOSSSH!!!

The Rolly Royce disappeared quickly. It left behind only a few giant bubbles. *Glug-glug.*

"Help! Help!" cried Norton. "My Rolly Royce! Well, don't just stand there!" he yelled at the police. "Do something!"

"Oh, we'll do something, all right," said Officer Piranha. What he did was burst out laughing. So did Officer Otter.

Norton was shouting and jumping up and down. That only made the police officers laugh harder.

I myself tried not to laugh. I didn't succeed. And honestly, I didn't try very hard.

I was still laughing when I got back home and told the story to Peccary.

"You should have seen the way his Rolly Royce sank into the Duck Pond," I told him. *"Glug-glug!"*

Peccary was helping me on with my white robe. I plopped down in my easy chair in front of the crackling fire and stuck out my feet. Peccary slipped on my red fuzzy slippers, Snuggly and Huggly. Home sweet home.

"Drink this, sir." Peccary handed me a mug of steaming cocoa.

"Mmm! With marshmallows! Peccary, you are a genius."

"I have always found hot cocoa to be just the thing after a brisk ride on a cold fall day, sir."

"Yes, indeed," I agreed. "Boy, it sure was cold. I guess it's because I had the top of the car—"

I screeched my words to a halt. Too late.

Peccary had an eyebrow raised. That big round pink nose of his was twitching slightly.

"Ah, Peccary?"

"Sir?"

"There's a bit more to the tale than I have taled you. I mean, *told* you."

"Oh?"

I proceeded to tell him everything that had happened *before* Norton's car rolled into the pond.

"But I only got a hundred-furthing fine," I said.

"That is surprisingly low, sir."

"For speeding. The hat over the face and the Hokey Pokey brought the total to three hundred."

"I see."

"Plus three hundred for dry cleaning their uniforms."

"Ah."

"Also, one of the police officer's horses stuck his head in my car and chewed my driving cap to pieces. I guess the orange color of the cap reminded the horse of carrots. I loved that driving cap, Peccary."

"I know you did, sir."

"But, Peccary, Norton lost his entire car. I would say I won that battle, wouldn't you?"

Peccary didn't answer.

I studied his face but I couldn't figure out what he was thinking.

"Finished with your cocoa?" he asked at last.

"Yes, thank you."

He took my empty mug and exited the living room.

"That was delicious," I called after him.

"I am glad to hear it, sir."

And that's it. This story ends rather happily, you see. In fact, it ends the way all my days end. That evening, Peccary drew me a warm bubble bath. He helped me into my jammies and tucked me into bed. Then he read me a chapter from my favorite adventure series, *The Constrictor Boys.* Tonight's book was called *The Badminton Bully.* I imagined Norton in the title role.

After Peccary read me the chapter, I begged for
more. Peccary, as always, said it was better to have
something to look forward to. But he did agree to
sing me a sea shanty he'd learned in the Navy. Lots
of "heigh ho" and "Raise the sails high, me heart-
ies." That sort of thing. Then he turned off the
light, said goodnight and left the room.

I list all of these activities in great detail because it was what Peccary *didn't* do that I appreciated most of all. Have you spotted it?

He never once said, "I told you so."

I could tell he was thinking it, though. Well, no butler is perfect, after all.

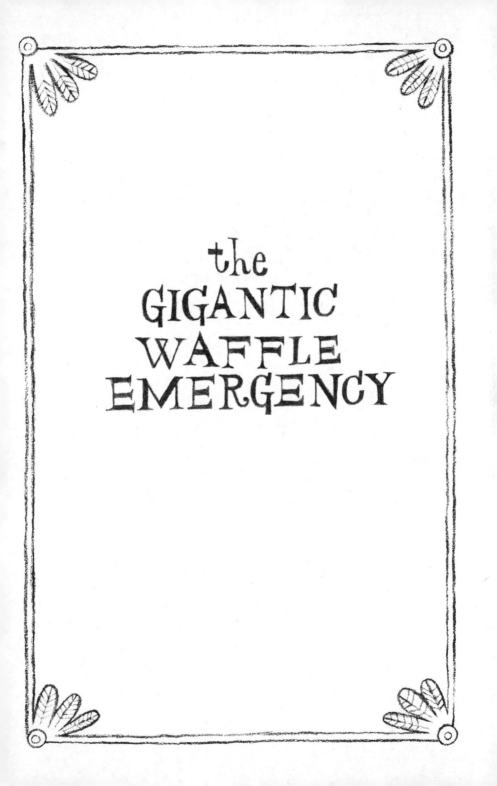

the
GIGANTIC
WAFFLE
EMERGENCY

One of the great things about living on my own is having my fine butler, Peccary, do everything for me. He keeps our little nest running shipshape. There's never a toy misplaced, never an item missing from the larder, never a speck of dust specking about. But on weekends I like to give the man a break. I motor down to the Coconut, my parents' home in the country, and let Mama and

Papa do everything for me instead. My dear old parents wait on me wing and foot.

One Saturday this past spring, my parents greeted me at the door, hugging me in what we like to call a "Parrott sandwich." But as they

The Coconut

were kissing me from both sides—*mwah! mwah! mwah!*—I noticed the old house had taken on a strange new odor. It was a smell with a bit of a sting to it. It made my eyes blink. My parents giggled with excitement while I sniffed.

"Is that . . . *waffles* I smell?" I really wasn't sure.

"Oh, Freddie, wait till you taste the batter," said Mama. "Your father has become quite the master chef, you know."

"Well, now," said my father modestly, as he patted his large belly.

"No, Papa, admit it. Freddie, I think this may be his greatest recipe yet."

"Well, now, I say again," said Papa, "I admit they are rather tasty. I made a triple batch last night. Your mother and I polished off the whole lot this morning."

"You had most of it," said my mother.

"Whatever. We have more than fifty guests coming to brunch in the morning. I had to whip up a truly gargantuan bowl. Come see."

"Yes, come, Freddie," said Mama. "You must taste it."

My parents tugged me to the kitchen. On the kitchen counter sat the biggest silver vat I'd ever seen. My father set out a step stool so I could climb up and peek down into the vat. The batter was pale and gloppy. It looked as if it had caught chicken pox. Purple acai berries floated everywhere.

The berries were not alone. Little peanut butter cups, mini-marshmallows, pretzels, candy canes and big chunks of butterscotch brownies stuck out from the surface.

"I tripled the sugar in the recipe," said my

father proudly. "My philosophy is that there is no such thing as too much of a good thing."

"Yes, Papa, that is your signature cooking style."

On the counter next to the vat sat a little family of condiments, two tall wooden salt and pepper shakers and a big jar of extra-spicy mustard. Flames decorated the jar's label.

"My waffles are both sweet and savory," said Papa proudly, when he saw where I was looking. "Go on, son," he urged me. "Taste the batter!"

"You won't believe how it tastes," said Mama.

"I bet I won't," I agreed. I scooped out the smallest bit of batter I could ladle. As I raised ladle to beak, my tongue curled back. Then I took my first taste.

I almost fell off the step stool.

The first chance I got I snuck into the hall and dialed Peccary.

"Mayday! Mayday!" I whispered.

"Yes, it is a May day, sir," Peccary agreed. "It is May thirteenth. And quite sunny and breezy."

"My dear Peccary," I said, "I know what day it is. That is not why I am calling."

"I see, sir. Well, it is certainly good to hear your voice, in any case."

Peccary sounded awfully jolly, I must say. Why, it was almost as if he were enjoying having a break from my company.

"What's all that splashing about I hear, Peccary? You're not taking one of those mud baths of yours, are you?"

"I am indeed, sir. Wonderfully cooling, sir."

"Well, I'm afraid you're going to have to stop cooling and come down to the Coconut at once. There is a huge waffle disaster brewing. And unless you come up with one of those genius plans of yours, my poor Papa will be utterly disgraced."

"Ah, there you are, Freddie!" said Papa, peeking around the corner. "Guess what, my boy! I made the waffles even better. I added bacon and fudge ripple ice cream."

"Fabulous," I told him. "Did you hear that?" I whispered to Peccary, when my father retreated back to his evil laboratory—I mean, the kitchen.

"I am beginning to sense your problem, sir,"

said Peccary. But the horrible man still sounded amused.

Just then, my mother came around the corner writing a new name on her guest list. "Guess who just agreed to come tomorrow?" she told me. "Sir Alex Horned Frog!"

"Sir Alex Horned Frog," I gasped. "As in, the world's foremost waffle expert?"

"Yes! Yes!"

"As in, the editor of *Waffles Magazine*?"

"The very one!"

"As in, the man who judged last year's national waffle contest?"

"Yes! Yes!" said Mama.

Sir Alex Horned Frog was known for his exquisite taste. He was also known for his nasty exposés when he tasted a waffle he felt was subpar. What would Sir Alex say about Papa's waffles? Poor Papa would be a national disgrace.

"Sir Alex Horned Frog," gushed Mama, clasping the guest list to her chest. "Oh, Freddie! Isn't it thrilling?"

"Utterly," I agreed.

With that, my mother left, humming and coo-
ing. I looked at the phone in my hand. I had forgotten I was talking to anyone. I lifted the receiver
to my ear.

"Hello?"

"I will catch the first train I can, sir," said Peccary.

"So, Peccary?" I said. "What's the plan?"

It was a little after nine that evening. I was sitting on the edge of my bed. The purple comforter, which has sat atop my bed my whole life, was supplying no comfort whatsoever.

Peccary had arrived at the Coconut only minutes before. Now he was sitting at my desk chair with his legs crossed and his eyes closed.

"I don't have a plan yet, sir."

"But you're thinking of one?"

"I'm thinking of one."

"You're thinking of one?"

"I'm thinking of one."

"You're thinking of—"

"Ah, sir, might I suggest a wee moment of silence? I find it to be an aid in the thinking process."

"Sorry. Think on, my friend, think on."

I should explain. When I get nervous I tend to repeat what other people say. It's the parrot in me, I suppose. It's the parrot in me, I suppose. There, you see?

Peccary slumped so far downward in the chair that his snout rested on his chest. Calmly he folded his well-manicured hands over his black-and-white-striped vest. He wrinkled his furry brow even more than usual. Air went into that big pink round nose of his ever so slowly, and it came back out at the same snail's pace. "Sssssss . . . sssssss . . . sssssss . . . sssssss . . . "

One might have thought he had fallen asleep, but I knew better. This was his deep-thinker pose, which he reserves for the toughest of problems. When he goes into these deep thinks of his, he

111

doesn't even hear me when I ask how his deep think is going.

"Peccary?" I said.

You see, no response.

I guess I had really stumped him this time. He was still sitting like a statue when my parents came to tuck me in for the night.

"Oh, dear? Is something wrong with Peccary?" whispered Mama. "He looks frozen."

"Oh, he's just got a little problem," I said.

"A problem?" gasped my father. "I hate those."

"Yes, but it's just a teeny-weeny one. And I'm sure he'll come up with a solution soon. Right, Peccary?"

To my surprise, Peccary opened his eyes. He stretched and yawned. "Oh, dear," he said, politely covering his mouth. "I guess that train trip really tuckered me out. Well, I'll say good night."

I gaped at him in horror. Was he going to bed without solving the waffle emergency?

"Oh, I almost forgot," he added casually, stopping at the door. "I thought I should warn you. Our Freddie here has developed a little health problem."

"Health problem?" my parents squawked, clapping their wings to their faces.

"Oh, it's nothing we can't handle," said Peccary. "In fact, it's only a problem if you happen to have any waffle batter in the house."

"Waffle batter?!" cried Mama and Papa.

"Yes," said Peccary. "You see, I'm afraid Freddie has developed a rare condition known as 'eating

waffles in your sleep.' But if there's no waffle batter in the house, you have nothing to fear."

"But I've made a huge new batch of batter for all of tomorrow's guests," said Papa. "We're having a waffle brunch."

"Oh, I see. Hmm. Yes. Well, then I must ask you to lock up the batter before you go to bed. Sweet dreams! And as I tell Freddie every night, don't eat the waffles!"

After Peccary left the room, Mama started moaning. "Oh dear, oh dear. My darling boy has come down with sleep-eating waffle disease."

I rubbed her shoulders. "Now, now, Mama. Don't worry. It will all come out all right in the end. At least, I hope so."

With so much to worry about, you might think I would have trouble falling asleep. Time to learn another of my great skills. I am a champion at falling asleep. Any time, any place. After my parents kissed me good night, I closed my eyes and I was out.

I woke to find myself locked in my room.

Peccary let me out at once. "Ah, good, you are up at last, sir."

"Why?" I asked, rubbing my eyes. "What time is it?"

"You have slept until three in the afternoon, sir. A new record. But now, if you will excuse me, I have some rather important business to attend to." He tapped his snout after he said this, which is one of his secret signals. Then he trotted briskly down the hall and out of sight.

I became aware of loud rumblings coming from downstairs. It sounded as if a herd of wildebeests had invaded the living room. I headed down the hall to the balcony. I saw the wildebeests. It was all my parents' friends and relatives in their best brunch suits and gowns. The guests were angrily and loudly chattering.

My old frenemy Norton called out, "Look! There he is! It's the sleep eater!" The whole crowd fell silent and looked up at me in a very unfriendly way.

Sleep eater? How did they find out about my sleep-eating habits?

My father was coming up the stairs. He had on his big white chef's hat, as well as his purple apron that says *I'M THE CHEF* in big white letters.

"Freddie," called Papa, "I told Mama not to tell anyone about your eating-waffles-in-your-sleep disease."

"Yes, you told me," agreed Mama, who was following Papa up the stairs. "But you whispered it so loudly that *everybody* heard!"

Mama was dressed in her sunflower dress, but the sunflowers were drooping. She was carrying a fizzy pink drink. "Tell them he's innocent," she told Papa.

"He's innocent, everyone!" said Papa.

"Nonsense!" grumbled the crowd. "He's guilty!"

"But how could he have eaten it?" Mama told the guests. "We locked him in his room all night."

"That's why," Papa told me, "when we discovered that the batter had been stolen, I called the police."

"The police?" I gulped.

Oh, dear. Whenever I get into a scrape, it always seems to be two particular police officers who arrive at the scene—on horseback.

A horse whinnied somewhere outside the house. There. You see?

"You're a pretty tricky waffle thief," called a familiar gruff voice. It sounded like Officer Piranha.

It *was* Officer Piranha. He was standing near the front door with his fins crossed over his blue-uniformed chest.

Next to him, her paws also crossed, was Officer Otter.

"The way we figure it," she said, "you musta climbed out your window."

"Right," agreed Officer Piranha. "You ate all the batter, every last drop of it. Then you climbed back into bed."

"Wait a minute! Do you mean to tell me that no one has so much as tasted your delicious waffles, Papa?" I said.

He shook his head sadly. "They didn't even get a whiff."

That's when it hit me like a flying waffle. I understood Peccary's plan! He had dumped the

batter and blamed it on me! And since I was asleep when I supposedly ate the waffles, how mad could the guests get?

From the way they were looking up at me, pretty mad.

Little bells chimed. Over by the mantel, below the large oil painting of me and my parents that looks nothing like us, stood my adorable Great Aunt Augusta. She was wearing her famous red felt hat, the one with twenty-six bells lettered A to Z. They are charms from her charm bracelet when she was four. She was waving her wings and jumping about. "Freddie! Freddie!"

"Auntie!" I waved back. It was so nice to see a friendly face amid a horde of furious ones.

"You poor darling!" called my aunt. "You must have been so hungry. But as your Auntie always says, there's no shame in having a good appetite! Is your stomach all right, dear?"

"It's fine, Aunt Augusta, thank you. I'm actually quite hungry."

This statement did not go over well with the brunch crowd. There was a lot of angry muttering. The general idea seemed to be that I shouldn't be

121

complaining about hunger. After all, I had eaten a giant vat of waffle batter in my sleep while they had had nothing to eat for hours.

"He'll be fine, Aunt Augusta," my mother said. "Here, Freddie, drink this." She handed me that fizzy pink drink she'd been carrying.

"Cheers, everyone!" I said, raising the glass. No one called cheers back. Then I took a sip and practically spat. "What is that?!"

"One of your father's latest inventions."

"It settles the stomach," Papa said proudly.

"I'll settle it later," I said, handing Mama back the glass. Papa looked hurt. "I promise," I added, trying to smile. "I'm sure it will work just great." He brightened.

I made a mental note. At my first opportunity I would dump the pink fizzy drink down the same hole Peccary had used to flush the waffle batter.

Someone cleared his throat. It sounded like a choo choo taking off from the station. All eyes turned.

In the center of the living room the crowd had made a space, like a spotlight. In the center of this space hulked the famous Sir Alex Horned Frog himself!

I'd never seen him in person before, only on the cover of magazines. He was wearing a lime-green tuxedo with shiny brass waffle buttons. His long wide mouth was turned down in a giant frown. His horns were twitching.

"Well, well, well," he said. "Now that we know what happened to the waffle batter, I'll be heading home. I'm so hungry I could faint."

Sir Alex turned toward the front door. Taking their cue from the waffle expert, the rest of the guests murmured that they had better be going, too. But just as the crowd began to move, the front door opened.

There stood Peccary! He was lugging that giant silver vat.

"I've found something that I believe will interest

all of you greatly," he told the crowd. With a grunt, he lifted the vat like a trophy. "Waffles!"

"Waffles!" cheered the crowd. Aunt Augusta raised her hat and jingled it.

"But, but—how did you—where did you?" joyously sputtered my father.

"It seems that Freddie only slept-ate a tiny bite of your batter, sir," Peccary explained. "That seems to be his pattern. Who can understand the mysterious ways of the sleep eater? He sleep-eats just a nibble, then hides the rest.

"Knowing his sleep-eating habits, I made a thorough search of the grounds. Just moments ago, I found the batter, safely stowed in the woodshed, where the chill air has preserved its freshness. Mr. Parrott, I think you will find your batter smelling and tasting just as waffly as ever."

"Hooray for Peccary!" roared the crowd. "Hip, hip, hooray!"

"Let's eat!" roared Sir Alex.

Peccary helped my parents lug the vat of batter to the kitchen. And before I knew it, we were all packed into the dining room, waiting to be fed.

Wait a minute! Why had Peccary brought back the batter? What on earth was he thinking? We were right back where we started, in an enormous waffle predicament.

"Waffles! Waffles!" chanted the guests, banging their silverware on the table.

The kitchen doors swung open. In streamed Peccary, Mama and Papa. They were carrying big silver trays of steaming waffles.

You could almost hear the guests' mouths watering. "Oooooh!" they cried.

"Now, I know we're all hungry," called Sir Alex from the head of the table, "but we must remember our waffle manners. We have to wait until everyone has been served."

With just one more kitchen trip my parents and Peccary served everyone. Including me.

In front of me on my plate sat the dreaded waffle. Acai berries, candy canes, pretzels, mini-marshmallows, peanut butter cups and bits of butterscotch brownie poked out the top and sides. The smells of mustard, fudge ripple ice cream and bacon mingled in my nares.

And what was this? Apparently my father had added yet another ingredient before locking up the batter: broccoli.

Peccary and my parents set out large glass pitchers of maple syrup. Pouring syrup is a quiet activity. For a moment, the only sounds were the clinking of glass on china and little whispers of "No, no, after you."

Next, the guests plopped dollops of whipped cream onto their waffles. It was so quiet you could hear a dollop plop.

The guests all looked at each other. Then everyone began slicing off their first bites of waffle. But then everyone stopped. All eyes were on the famed waffle judge and expert, Sir Alex Horned Frog. Everyone was waiting for the great man to take his first bite.

Sir Alex forked a bite of waffle into his long, long mouth.

Slowly he chewed.

A chew to the left.

A chew to the right.

Gulp!

He swallowed.

A peculiar look came over the man's broad light-green face.

Then he smiled.

"Magnificent," he said.

"But how, Peccary? How did you do it?" I was sitting on the edge of my seat, which was the edge of my bed.

Peccary smiled. When he didn't answer at once, I started kicking the footboard and chanting, "Tell me! Tell me!"

Downstairs, the brunch was still going strong. Nobody could get enough of Papa's waffles! I had dragged Peccary up to my room so he could explain his magic trick.

"C'mon, Peccary. Fess up. When and how did you make the new batter?"

"The new batter, sir?"

"Peccary, I ate one of those waffles. I loved it!"

"I believe you had seven of them, sir."

I laughed. "But that proves my point. Those waffles are delicious. I mean, I admit I was absolutely starving. I probably would have enjoyed eating wood chips. But come now, Peccary, tell me your secret. How did you turn my father's waffles into such tasty treats?"

"You have already solved the mystery yourself, sir."

"I *have*?"

"It has been hours and hours since any of your guests have eaten, sir. Hunger is the best sauce."

Ah, Peccary. The man is truly a genius, is he not? He saved the brunch and the Parrott family name. And the next morning, I was back at my own dining room table, where I can always count on breakfast to taste just right.

About the Author

As a TV writer and producer, Eric Daniel Weiner cocreated and produced several of preschool television's most successful series, such as the smash hit *Dora the Explorer*. *The Famously Funny Parrott* is his debut children's book.

ericdanielweiner.com

About the Illustrator

Brian Biggs has illustrated dozens of books over the last twenty years, covering a range of subjects. While he has drawn cars and trucks, robots, leprechauns, dinosaurs, kittens, trains, monsters, aliens, and bridges for books, this is the first opportunity he has had to illustrate a book about a parrot.

brianbiggs.com